EROTIC
REFLECTIONS VOL 1

author

Hay Z Mae

CONTENTS

FROM THE AUTHOR:

First, I want to say thank you for your support. This is my first published project and it is raw from beginning to end. I made mistakes and left them there so that as my journey to becoming the best author possible continues I can look back and see just how far I have come. The goal is to always make my next project, my best project.

Please know that these stories are fantasy based. Any resemblances to a real person, location, or event is unintentional.

From cover to cover you will find juicy, risqué short stories as well as sensual poetry, all of which were written by me. I have always had a passion or writing and found Erotic pieces as a way to express myself as I stepped into womanhood. Enjoy !

ISBN: 9781079372229

THE SHOOT OUT

Its noon and this is the first chance I've gotten all day to check my phone. I scrolled pass the three missed calls from my sister, my best friend, and my momma to respond to the double text from Zay bae. Now before you question my judgement let

me explain to you how fine Isaiah Davenport is. The epitome of Black excellence, he owns a gym downtown and he couldn't have chosen a more fitting career. He's 5'11, a solid 200 pounds. You wouldn't know he's hiding tattoos from collar bone to belly button under that tailored 3 piece suit. Add in his full beard, his dimples & his smile the Lord sculpted this man by hand. Looking at him is enough to warm my honey pot. Anyway, his first text said "Wassup birthday girl" his second text said "If you don't already have plans come over. We can order something to eat and finish that Netflix series." I responded "Hey, I should be free around 730 pm, I can come over then." He sends back "That works".

Finally off work, I stop by the store. Oddly enough only food lion carries the two bottles of wine I really like so I stop there first because it is right across the street from my job. I grab 2 bottles of wine, both of which are truly for me because he rarely ever finishes one cup. He usually enjoys 2 beers to my full bottle of wine.

I drive home to throw somethings in my overnight bag and I am in an exceptionally good mood. Singing along to my personalized apple music station. At this age birthdays are just another day, before I got his text I was probably going to take myself to go eat or sit home on the phone with my best friend watching shows together and comparing our lives to fictional television characters like Issa Rae and Meridith Grey. Though I do enjoy all of those things, it goes without saying that I am pleasantly surprised to receive a text from Isaiah, he never disappoints.

I met him on tinder days after my job moved me to this city and we have been tight ever since. In fact it has been about two years now and I don't recall a time we've gone more than a month without talking. Even if we aren't actively fucking on each other I know I can call him when my car isn't starting or I need help putting together whatever unnecessary item I bought for my place.

If I can recall correctly our friendship has withstood 4 of his "relationships". Now I don't want to sound full of myself and say that most of those ended on account of me but uh most of his females weren't feeling the idea of us being as close as we are. To top off their insecurity he flirts as well as he breathes, it is just who he is! If his warm brown eyes and benevolent smile wasn't alluring enough his personality would certainly seal the deal with any woman he went after.

Needless to say I'm content with spending my birthday having sex and falling asleep to whatever 2 star Netflix movie he chooses. We just started this "Friends with Benefits" thing about 8 months ago. Its sporadic, when we both have the chance to enjoy each other, we do. We have a very unconventional relationship accompanied by an indescribable bond. What we consider friends with benefits other people may think is completely out of line.

There have been times when we are together every

day and all night for a month straight then life happens and we may not see each other for 2 weeks. No issues there because we aren't in a relationship meaning there is really no expectations. The lines are clear, the arrangement we have works for the both of us. Should either of us decide we no longer wish to continue, we can bow out gracefully and remain friends. I just got out of a relationship that I wasted over two years on and it ended terribly when my job offered me a position in a new city. When I decided I was ready for companionship again I realized I was not ready for all that a relationship brings, so I made a tinder. With his business being 24 hours he doesn't exactly have time to maintain a stable relationship anyway. This works for us!

I usually have my overnight bag on standby in the trunk for moments such as these but I used it last time I crashed at my best friend's house. Engaged in small talk with my mom about the party she through for me when I turned 10, as I walk around the room tossing things on the bed. My cosmetic bag which is filled with all the essentials, from a tooth brush to unscented bar soap and a travel size container of body wash, as well as emergency tampons because mother nature is a sneaky, evil heffa. Two pair of underwear and a bra. A grey sweat suit with a large navy blue check on the front, my navy blue air max plus and a pair of black ankle socks. My MacBook, a phone charger, my bonnet, a face rag, ass rag and a towel. After doing a brief inventory of my items I throw them in the oversized black and silver Victoria secret tote bag and make my way to the door.

I spent the the entire 45 minute drive to his house returning phone calls I missed throughout the day. Making plans to meet up with my mother and my sister this weekend to get some food and meet my best friend at our favorite happy hour spot. Finally I turn on his street and call his phone.

"Hey, I'm here. Come downstairs."

"Yes ma'am" and ends the call.

After finding a parking spot he comes to grab my duffle bag and I grabbed my bag from the gas station.

We get in the house I put the wine on the counter and take my duffle bag to the bedroom to shower. One of the joys of our arrangement is that he isn't my man, and I'm not trying to make him my man so I don't exhaust unnecessary effort trying to impress him. I've realized he gives me the same dick if I'm here in heels and a thong, as he does if I have a 2XL t shirt. He says "it all looks the same on   the   floor."

So after spending what he considers an absurd amount of time washing off the remnants of my day, I return to the living room. Clean as well as comfortable, dressed in a black t shirt I found in the drawer where he stores old graphic tees, black

Nike socks and black underwear. I grab the remote and take a seat on the couch. Scrolling through the tv guide in an effort to find something worth watching while he does whatever he is doing in the kitchen. Periodically yelling out movie titles and reading the description out loud only for him to give me the same answer, no, in a different way. Eventually I lose all hope and select BET because no one ever gets tired of watching baby boy.

Eventually I make my way to the kitchen to grab my wine and make a selection from the drawer of take out menu's he keeps stashed next to the fridge. To my surprise he is cooking, well finishing up. Chicken parm with angel hair noodles and garlic knots that he picked up from the Italian spot up the street.

Now typically home cooked meals does not come with the "Friends with Benefits" package but like I said our arrangement does not follow the "normal" guidelines at all. We eat dinner while watching standup comedy on Netflix. Completely content with ending the night as is I get up to put our dishes in the kitchen and return to curl under the cover on my end of the couch. He rubs his hands up and down my leg to ensure I'm not falling asleep before he slides into the kitchen.

Moments later he returns singing the off key Stevie Wonder rendition of Happy Birthday, holding a

Caramel cupcake that has one lit candle in the middle of it. At this point I'm standing up doing my "happy I love food dance". I haven't been able to go to the bakery that makes my favorite Salted Caramel Pretzel cupcakes in months because they are always closed by the time I get off work and make it to this side of town. He finishes singing and I blow the candle out. I instantly take one huge bite of the cupcake and a finger swipe the icing that was falling off the side before I sit it on the table. Straddling him in the middle of the couch I kiss his cheek and thank him for spending my birthday   with   me.

He returns the kiss and stands up with me wrapped around him. With his hands on my ass and my legs clinched around his waist we never stopped kissing

for the 30 steps it took to get from the living room

to his bed. Laying me on the bed he kneels at the

end of the bed with his chin resting near my belly

button he looks up smiling "We can't end your

birthday like that" he laughs before kissing me.

With no hesitation he swiftly removed my panties

and placed a tender kiss on my pussy lips. Resting

my legs on his shoulders, with my head thrown

back and my right hand on the back of his neck I

inhale deeply. Rolling the tip of his tongue around

my clit he slides one hand up my shirt and

squeezes my breast. Rhythmically switching from

slow swirls to rapid flicks of his tongue against my

clit. My legs trembling was all the proof he needed that he was on the right track.

Moments later my whole body stiffens as I let out what can be best be described as more of a squeal than a moan. Being the over achiever that he is making me cum does not mean stop so he continues at this pace until I push on his shoulders and put my legs down hard enough for him to back away. He stands up licking what remains of me from his lips and staring into what is left of my soul the entire time.

Dropping his basketball shorts exposing his manscaped penis he leans in and kisses me. My left hand wrapped around his back, grabbing his dick with my right I stroke it twice. He kisses my neck as I rub his dick against my pussy lips. The tip of his dick grazed my warmth and caused him to let out a "mmmm" that I'd never heard from him before. His body is pressed against mine he thrusted and entered me, raw. We are both aware that unprotected sex is not smart and definitely not what "Friends with Benefits" do. Before today we always used condoms, I'm not on birth control and neither of us want to be new parents in the peak of our careers.

This was new! He hovers over me delivering slow but steady strokes. My moans and his grunts are almost in sync as he glides in and out of me. Now that we have gotten acclimated the gentle strokes turn to powerful thrust.

In what I'm sure is an effort to not cum too fast he stops stroking and commands me to turn around. I do as I am told and flip over on all fours. With my hands out in front of me as if I was going to do a push up, my toes hang off the edge of the bed and I spread my knees allowing him direct access. He wraps both his hands around the front of my neck and dives into me. Getting deeper and deeper, he smacks my ass and I drop my face into the mattress and let out a scream. Pulling at the corner of the bed I managed to inch my way to the middle of the bed. Determined to fight back I arch my back and use the little strength I have left to throw

my ass at him.

Impressed but determined to win he pulls his dick

out and replaces it with his tongue. Taken by

surprise I let out a moan and he wrapped his hand

around me and removed any ability I had to run.

He rises and pushes his hands on the small of my

back forcing me to my stomach. Spread out like a

starfish with my face burrowed into the mattress, I

already know the kind of trouble I can get in when

he has me in this position, but I'm ready.

Defenseless and seconds from an orgasm he

shoves his dick back inside me. All 8 inches of

him filled my insides in a way I cannot even

describe. Judging by the change in the tempo of his strokes I can tell he's about to cum. With both hands resting right above my ass he drills into me faster and harder and lets out a loud growl. While waiting for him to return with the wet rag I struggled to catch my breath. Eventually he comes back in the room and admits he made no attempt to pull out because I deserve to have the club shot up on my birthday.

A NIGHT IN PARIS

Leave it to Jace to try and sneak in a few strokes while everyone is watching the fight. This wouldn't be the first time we had sex with a house full of guest downstairs so we knew we had to be careful. Extra careful, like when you're 52 weeks deep in someone's Instagram trying not to like a picture on accident, that kind of careful!

"I have a surprise for you" I whispered in his ear while he kissed my neck. "Really right now? I'll be quick, just let me hit it from behind"… "Wait, I promise you will want this surprise now". I assure him as I adjust my dress and walk out the bedroom and back downstairs. After about four agonizing minutes I return to the room with a gift he had been asking for since our 3rd wedding anniversary.

"Hold on, I'm confused." He looked back and forth from me to her.

"I thought this was a friend from work that you invited to watch the fight?"

"Well, I lied. She is handpicked for us" I respond with a smirk on my face.

With the biggest smile on his face he turned the tv up and took off his shirt. Completely aware that I still admire beautiful women and have enjoyed them in the past he has never actually seen me with a woman. I have never wanted to share my husband with another woman but the idea of having the affection and delicacy of a woman as well as the dominance and aggression of a man is a fantasy I could not wait to live out.

He attentively watches me run my fingers through her loose curls, kissing her while she rubs her hands up my thigh. It has been almost four years since I have been with a woman. That probably has a lot to do with the fact that since we met it has been just us.

Our 3 year marriage anniversary is a few weeks away, valentine's day. If you're doing the math and raising an eyebrow yes we did get married within a few months of knowing each other. When you know you know! Nothing about our relationship has been traditional, including this moment. I've debated with myself for months now, since he proposed the idea.

He didn't press me about it which probably contributed to me actually considering it. We were having a conversation about sexuality and discussed my few times I had been involved with a female. Neither of us have ever had a threesome and the idea of me enjoying him and a woman at the same time was exhilarating. I think that he fantasizes about the bisexual side of me a lot, he has so many questions. We discussed the similarities in our "type" when it comes to women. We both like extremely girly women, the bouncy curls, and long legs. Long nails, kind of high maintenance and a naturally pretty face.

The glazed look in his eyes made putting this surprise together worth all the stress. It has proven to not be as easy as I first imagined to find a woman who meets all my requirements. She had to be single, someone both of us would find attractive. Willing to have a one night stand, no string attached, no desire to reach out to us afterwards. Someone who didn't know a lot of the same people we know and also comfortable sharing her STD test results with a stranger.

After some help from a fake tinder I made months ago, I had narrowed my five options down to just two women. After arranging to sit down with both of them I thought my decision was made. However I ended up with my number two because the chocolate girl with almost no waist line and a whole lot of ass was sure to give us a great time but she rightfully refused to show proof that she was on some form of birth control and has been recently tested for all STD's.

Here we are, a week short of three years since we got married and I am inviting another woman into our bedroom. To make things a little more interesting I arranged it for a day when all of our closest friends would be over for the fight we agreed to host months ago. Unfortunately I had to drag my best friend into this ordeal to ensure she could stop any and every one from leaving the basement for anything while we snuck off.

I had the timing almost perfect as the opening events kicked off I made sure everyone had everything they needed. A table lined the back wall with every sports event dish you could think of. 200 wings in 5 different flavors, buffalo chicken dip, cheese sticks, fried pickles, and meatballs. Not to mention the fully stocked bar we just recently got installed in our basement. After playing hostess and making sure all of my guest were comfortable, drunk and stuffed I set my plan into motion.

I asked Jace to run upstairs and make sure all the kids were alright and still sleeping peacefully. Moments after he went up the stairs I send a text and Kera starts making her rounds saying how she had to go for whatever made up reason she came up with. Once she was gone and everyone was settled in I snuck off.

Fast forward to this moment, I'm kissing this peanut butter colored girl with shoulder length curls and unstrapping her bra to free her plump C cup breast. Jace gets up to lock the bedroom door without ever taking his eyes off of us. I've already removed her shirt and I'm planting tender kisses from her lips down to her navel. She lays back allowing me to remove her jeans and I rest her legs on my shoulders. Jace stands there with his arms crossed watching for a moment as I prove just how into women I am. I kneel at the edge of the bed and dance my tongue along her clit. She squirmed and moaned reassuring me that after all this time, I still got it.

Finally ready to join in he steps out of his sweat pants and removes his white t shirt. I stand up and kiss my husband passionately to let him taste her from my lips. We engage for so long almost forgetting she was there until she dropped to her knees in front of us. She finds a place for his dick in her throat while actively moving her fingers inside me. We move to the bed and I position myself on all fours with him standing behind me and her laying on the bed directly in front of me. I enjoy the sweetness that is her, while my husband sends back shots up my spine.

In an effort to not waste the experience I suggest we change positions. Jace lays on his back horizontally on the bed and I assume my position on the dick with my feet grounded to the bed. Kera looks at me for approval before riding my husband's face. I nod in affirmation and she leans in to kiss me. I never could have imagined the amount of core strength I was required to have in order to ride dick and make out with a woman who was less than 2 feet away.

As I'm struggling to maintain some sort of rhythm, Kera is almost crumbling at the works of Jaces tongue. We lock hands and bridge them in the air for added support, for a second we formed an Eiffel Tower trying to hold each other up. We change positions and I lean back against the headboard while Kera puts her ass in the air and her face between my thighs. Jace drills her from behind while never taking his eyes off me. She clearly has been with a woman before because her pussy eating skills are immaculate! I clench my arms behind her head as we both moan out in ecstasy. Jace pulls out and positions himself at the head of the bed where I'm leaning. I put him in my mouth and taste every bit of her and him combined. I work my hands and my tongue in unison until he starts to buckle at the knees.

After being with him for so long I know all this signs that he's about to cum. I spin my tongue around the tip of his dick until I hear the "ahhhh fuck" followed directly by his release. He collapsed on the bed while Kera and I share one last kiss before disappearing into the bathroom together.

I retrieve two rags from the bathroom closet and run warm water over both of them. I give one to Kera and take the other one to my husband who is still laying across the bed with his eyes closed. I wipe everything from the base to the tip twice before taking the rag back into the bathroom. I run more warm water over the rag and use it to wipe myself clean. I brush my teeth and adjust my ponytail before throwing my dress back on and giving Jace his clothes. Kera smiles at us again before I escort her to the door never to be seen or heard from again.

I return only to find Jace still spread out across the bed in complete euphoria I pass him his clothes and encourage him to put them back on. "We have to go back downstairs", I reminded him in between soft kisses on his cheek. "We have to go entertain our guest."

I know you're probably thinking who sneaks to have sex in their own house? Can't they just wait? But sneaking it that much more fun.

I caught my husband giving me the eye in between yelling at the TV. As if we didn't just have threesome less than an hour ago he's still sitting across the room looking at me like a pink starburst out the wrapper. I love this man so much, here's to another memory to log in our mental scrapbook that relives our love story. I'll remember this moment as the time we visited the Eiffel Tower without ever leaving our house!

<u>Appetite</u>

I didn't know I was starving until I tasted you....
I want every drop of your sweetness, there will be no wasted juice....
Let them believe what they may but i promise to tell no lies.
Pulling, choking, and smacking until my soul cries....

Publicly we're platonic, but privately we're into pleasin.
Foreplay is just an appetizer because we're not into teasin…
You like the tattoos on my legs but even more what's between it. I walk past, you grab my ass I'm wondering it they seen it…..

Strip me of all my clothes and I'll be dressed in anticipation.
The meal is always worth, the amount of time you kept me waiting

Music is low, I wanna hear the noises you going make.
Scratch me and scream as much as you want, I ain't stopping til you shake.

Famished for your flesh, every piece of you I'll devour.
Your body is my buffet, all I can eat in the next hour.

I come here when I'm starving and every time my orders the same. && every time my meal is ready I enjoy it with no shame…

Now, its been a minute, when's the next meal, I can't wait.
You know every time you serve it up, ima always clean my plate

The Treatment

Treat her like your queen but fuck her with some disrespect.
Tell her what you're going then put your hands around her
neck.

Nibble on her ear, and pin her knees to her chest & make sure
she gets hers first then you can freestyle with the rest.

Trail kisses down her spine & then drill her into submission.
Turn her around, put it in her stomach because that's what
she's been missing.

She's a princess out in public but a slut behind closed doors.
See if she still got that same energy when she's pinned down
on all fours.

Let her work it on top & then stroke her from behind. I bet she
has two heart beats every time you cross her mind.

Round after round. Who going quit first.
Beat it til she sore, I love how it hurts.

Whoever loses gets the rag, that's the rule you got to know.
And if we just friends who like fuckin then you know, you
gotta go.

Can't wait for the next time, I'll see you again next week.
Head so good I won't be quiet but the dick so good I can't
speak.

You talked all that shit but your eyes rolled back, I seen it.
And in case this is your only chance, you better fuck me like
you mean it.

STALLING

Every third Tuesday of the month I come to this bar with my girls. Only place in town where we can enjoy some drinks, hookah if we want, and they host an open mic night. Nisa, Kaylin and I were 3 pitchers in when you took the stage. Rich chocolate skin, skinny covered in tattoos with locs resting on your shoulders, you caught my attention before you said a word. Whoever wasn't already captivated by your looks was drawn in by your voice. Performing a piece written on a subject I'm sure you know all too well, intimacy!!

The way the words rolled off your tongue I could almost taste them. The way you described the inner workings of a woman's body and the different ways to please her. The way you looked almost every female in the eyes as you performed. This was not my first time seeing you, but I would make sure it was the last time I let us leave as strangers. You finish your performance, the whole room erupts into claps, whistles, cheers and smirks from the dozen other women in the room you just seduced. I knew you and Kay work together so I figured you would eventually stop by our table. I was right, you walk up to our table wave to Nisa and I before turning your hat backwards and leaning in to hug Kaylin. I don't know what you're wearing but it lingered when you walked away. While the next performer goes, we engage in the most intense nonverbal conversation I have ever had.

Eventually the now 4 pitchers we have consumed gets to me and I wander off into the bathroom. The door just barely closes behind me before you walk in. Fixated on the way you lick your lips before you start talking I found myself wondering if the piece you performed was fact or fantasy.

"I don't want to come off like a predator but I feel like you wanted me to follow you" you proclaim as you lean against the door. Without even opening my mouth I confirm your assumption. You lock the door. I am ever so glad I wore this strapless bodycon dress today. Brazen and tipsy I'm sitting on the sink with my dress pulled down to my bellybutton.

You walk over and grab my hair tugging it to the left leaving my neck exposed.
"Are you nervous? You ask as you place a soft kiss on near my collar bone.
"I can hear your heart beating" I nod my head in confirmation.

Things escalate from you sucking on my neck to us kissing while you squeeze one of my nipples. I am sure it was a combination of your performance, the ridiculous amount of drinks I chugged and the fact my friends and I decided to experiment with some pills that has me more than ready to go.

You slip your fingers inside me and I can hear my juices splashing on your hand. Kneeling in front of the sink you push my legs further apart and my dress pops up. Completely exposed and dripping wet I grab the back of your head and push your face into my pussy. I've never had my pussy ate so masterfully!

My grip on your locs keeps getting tighter and I am sure everyone outside the door can hear me moaning. Just as I am about to cum you stop and stand up putting one hand over my mouth and the other back inside me. We lock eyes and you start fingering me rapidly until I cream all over your fingers.

I'm breathing heavily and staring at myself in the mirror when I realize the pills made me hallucinate and I have been in this bathroom alone the whole time. I wash my hands, readjust my dress, and apply some lip gloss before heading back to our table.

DINING IN

Sex is easily comparable to food. In the way that everyone is responsible for maintaining a healthy appetite that best suits them. I had no idea I had been starving until I met him!

Before I met him I was getting all the basic food groups, nothing spectacular but it got the job done! As a 22 year old woman I was tired of being a vegetarian. I'm excited to try some new food, and expand my pallet a little. For a while I established an eating disorder, binge eating with no regard for portions or what those habits would do to my body. Eventually I realized the temporary satisfaction of those foods was not worth the potential health risk I could be facing later. Choosing to slow down on my own accord, I decided it was time to start looking for a chef. After what seemed like forever without a good meal I found him. The chef my kitchen longed for. He was good with his hands, masterfully moved around the kitchen and most importantly had a clean record.

This chef uses spices and recipes that I never could have imagined. This chef has changed my appetite completely.

Now I found I like my pleasure with an equal serving of pain. The excitement that brewed inside of me while anticipating what new dish he would introduce me to was enough to make me crumble.

First he incorporated some choking, not the borderline homicidal choking you see in porn but one that matched the strength of his strokes. Initially it took a second for me to determine if I enjoyed this and he could tell but the moment he took his hand away I placed it right back.

For the next meal he made choking merely an appetizer. Like any good chef he is equipped with a plethora of utensils. Ones I have never seen! For example the adjustable metal latch bar that can be strapped at my wrist or my ankles....

Agreeing to the ankles and a blind fold I had no idea what his intentions were but I was confident I would enjoy whatever was on the menu for tonight.

"If you change your mind at any time, and you can, I need you to clap your hands. Words and tones are easily misunderstood in this setting but if you clap I'll know to stop. Understand?"

"Yes, got it" you could hear the nervousness in the way my voice.

He pulled me off the bed and guided us to a lounge chair in the corner of the room. I sat down and he kneeled at my feet, first he placed the straps on each ankle and adjusted the bar to the next to highest setting. Leaving my legs spread like a jumping jack. He waited for some sign of agreement before grabbing the blind fold. Pulling my hands so I would stand up, he instructed her to turn around. I did and bent over at the hips with my elbows resting on the back of the chair.

He spread my cheeks and as a token of gratitude for the wax I received two days prior, he ate it from the back, vigorously, until she started to buckle at her knees.

He stood up and filled me with his firm dick. Inhaling deeply as he served his first stroke. He let me be sure I liked it before asking how the meal taste. "Good, so good" I replied with no breath in between & her eyes closed. "I thought so" he confidently retorted.

He smacked her ass and kept stroking then something happened. The rhythm of his strokes changed and she could tell he was moving around a lot more. Suddenly, the flavor changed and things became a little more spicy. He was penetrating both my holes but it wasn't a thumb. I'd had that before. This was something longer, and spiraled. It felt amazing!! Gliding in and out of me at the same rhythm as his strokes. I let out 3 simultaneous "mmmm" "omg"s .... holding onto my waist with his free hand he kept me balanced while serving me this full course meal all by himself! The man is talented!!!

CLOUD 9

Why would he think it's okay to be knocking on this door at 330 in the morning? Rushing to the door before my neighbor wakes up, utterly annoyed but far from surprised by the audacity of my ex-boyfriend to show up uninvited.

He had been sending text messages and snap chats for the last 2 hours, clearly intoxicated, expressing his desire to make things right. Facetiming me trying to stroll down memory lane about how good our makeup sex always was. Paying him no mind, I responded with only dry one word answers and emojis. I just got off the phone with my best friend earlier laughing about how you let a dude get away with a little more than you usually would when the sex is fire. Shawn is proof!

We haven't been together in over a year but somehow THIS keeps happening. I'm just going to have to move when I do decide to move on because I'm sure the next person I date will not appreciate his impromptu visits at the ass crack of dawn. I guess the only reason we even still communicate is because we didn't have a bad break up and the sex is amazing!

With my only choices being to leave him pounding on my door for the whole complex to hear, or bring him inside to save myself the humiliation, I let him in. He was visibly drunk. I am not even sure how he got here but I sure hope he did not drive. Attempting to guide him to a seat, proved nearly impossible since he is about six foot even and around 240 pounds to my 5'3. He's mumbling about how he knows I love him and we belong together. I'm not acknowledging any of it! All of this is all too familiar because it happens almost routinely every 2-3 months, whenever he gets drunk and realizes he lost me.

We go in my room and he sits on the end of the bed with his feet hanging off. I lean back against the pillows with one leg tucked under me. The Hennessy encouraged him to run his hand up and down my leg and to his surprise I didn't stop him as he started feeling all up my inner thighs. He took that as the invitation to do as he pleased.

He slid his hand up the tshirt I was wearing and went right for the prize. He ran two fingers overtop of my panties warning me of where we was going. I through my head back and took a deep breath in. Holding my panties to the side with one hand, he leaned in, and dove face first into my candy pit. As soon as his tongue touched my clit I let out a moan, which only enticed him to show off more. He swirled his tongue in circles and I remember why I put up with his shit for so long. He lays down sniper style on the bed and I hold behind my knees keeping my legs spread like a peace sign.

With one hand inside me, the faster he flicked his tongue the stiffer my legs became…

The entire time he's giving me head I can hear my phone ringing but it is the last thing on my mind right now. He came up for air and we kissed for a while before I slid my hands down the front of his boxers.

I stroked it for a second and licked my lips before sticking his dick as far down the back of my throat as I could. I wrap my lips around the tip of his dick while one hand strokes the rest. Looking up I get all the confirmation I need because I see his eyes closed and his mouth wide open!

The more I gag the sloppier it gets. I have my right hand cuffed around his dick and work my mouth and my hands as a team until I see his stomach cave in. Confidently performing some of my best work, with spit running down my hands, I know he is about to erupt. We lock eyes and he cups his hand beneath my chin to free himself from my grip.

He pulls me up and turns me around. With one leg on the ground and one leg on the bed, I clench the sheets because I know what's to come. He starts by rubbing his tip against my lips as a courtesy greeting before pushing his pole into my flower pit. Penetrating parts of me that had not been touched since the last time we fucked for the last time.

My phone has been ringing nonstop since we started but I will not walk away from all this to see who is calling me at this time of night, I'll return their call in the morning.

He continues stroking me gently from behind and then picks me up. Suspended in the air, . As intoxicated as he is, he somehow manages to hold me up and continue serving long, deep strokes while I hold on to his neck for support. Calling out his name as I clench my legs tighter and tighter around his waist I feel him start to shake as if he's about to cum. his arm is wrapped around my body holding me close to him, I place my chin on his shoulder and climax at the same time as him.

Laying on the bed basking in all their after sex glory, it sounds like someone is using the key to come in the house. My best friend burst in the door, to let us know that Shawn's drunk ass never ended his facebook live.

We look over at the night stand only to realize his phone is propped up against his wallet giving the internet audience a front row seat to our show. Everything we just did has already gone viral.

Maybe this was the sign I needed that it was definitely time to leave him the hell alone for good. I'm sure it was screen recorded and uploaded onto the cloud! Any time I want to relive what we shared I could just log onto facebook and

see it shared all up and down my newsfeed.

Mind Fucked

I'm in love with you because you lie the best, reading
the writing on my inner walls, rearranging my
stress.... your words glide smoothly across my mind,
carving your name in my chest! You've been
blessed....

With the pieces need to take me places I've never
been..&& like a broken washing machine I'm stuck
on final spin. . .

Between I love you & I should leave ... I lock the door
then give you the keys...because no matter how bad
things get between us, you fix it between my knees.

Now even though sex started this whole thing, it's
turned into so much more... you've peaked into the
window of my soul & opened so many doors.....

The sweet love that we make can't undo the toxicity
of our relations.. so I'll have to continue making love
to you, in my imagination....

<u>Fuck Boy Fetish</u>

Fighting off the fuck boy fetish I got.
You know the boy who fucks you so good you
think it's love and it's not.

Everybody knows fuck boys come with good dick
and lots of stress. Like each stroke fills you with
frustration while he sucks your sanity from your
breast.

<u>*Lucid*</u> dreams, that always end the same. How
could my skull be this thick? Or is my entire
memory of all the bullshit erased each time I
bounce on the dick?

Addicted to the sensation of you, your lips are in
control of my nerves. Weakened when your fingers
touch my skin, you're in control of my curves.

What's the cure for curiosity because that internal
beast doesn't shut up til you feed it. For now I'll
use up all my batteries and tell myself I DONT
NEED IT

STRANGERS

I've been trying to play nice but my patience is
sparse.
I let you play with my pussy, you chose to play
with my heart.
You're ungrateful, & you're broken.
Don't even remember the last time we spoke and..
That's how we should keep it!!

CAUTION

Lately I've been a little apprehensive, causing me
to be more cautious with who my time is given to.
My sanity was amongst the last of things I'd give
to you.
I'm protecting my peace, keeping you out of my
sheets. You're a cannibal, a beast.
On my vulnerability you feast. But at least....
I learned to be a little more careful

CURVED

Turn her around, pin her down. She going bite her
lip.
Choke her while you stroke her, she going like that
shit.

Eyes in the back of my head, juices running down
your chin.
You better reach for that rubber before you try to
put it in.

Wet covers, nasty lovers. You a little too deep.
Rubber in the trash, warm water on the rag. Now
we going to sleep.

Wake up and eat it. Go to sleep then repeat it.
I like when you taste it, but I *LOVE* when you beat
it.

Face down, on all fours. Late nights, unlocked
doors.
Stay the night I want more. That's enough, now
she's sore.

You really no good for me but that curve got me
hooked.
Temptation got me, I'm just glad it's as good as it
looked.

PLAN B

Frantically throwing clothes in bins and shoving shirts into my dresser drawers to clear up the pile of clean laundry I have been avoiding for days now. I replace the wax in the scensy sitting on my bathroom sink and on my living room window seal before I turn on my sound bar. Running a shower and realizing I have 30 minutes before he gets here. Performing a duet with Trey Songs while I tend to my love flower and shave my legs.

Let me back up a little and explain why I'm last minute prepping for a dick appointment. After dragging around Satan's waterfall for about a week, I found myself hornier than usual. It has been about 3 months since I cut ties with my supplier and up until now I have been able to satisfy myself. Today I called on bedside Bob and that wasn't enough, so I accepted what I needed could not be obtained from my battery operated boyfriend. I want sex so good that I put my soul in a rubber maid container for him to take home with him. The warmth of another body pressed against mine, kisses that trail from my collar bone to my knee cap and everywhere in between. I needed a dick appointment.

After browsing through my mental rolodex of big dick bandits I realized I am trying to refrain from reigniting any of my old flames. Dave always brings me food but he likes to stay the night after every fuck, Chris fucks too good and I might catch feelings again, and Jason has a girlfriend according to Facebook so I guess I'll try out someone new.

After consulting with my best friend on FaceTime for 15 minutes we agreed my best bet was to give Grayson a call. Not that I'm interested in starting over with someone new and learning someone all over again but a girl has needs. We will both enjoy getting this one off and go back to exactly what we were before. Nothing has to change. I'm not hiring, but we can pretend this is an interview for a newly vacant temp slot.

Grays and I have known each other a few months but he is for everybody so I had convinced myself to leave him where he was. We have hung out a few times, had a handful of half decent conversations and I even let him spend the night a few times. I know there is a pinch of chemistry or at least we enjoy each other's company. He usually only gets invites to come kick it when I'm on my period or when I wanted male company. I called him to make sure there is no confusion about what this visit is for though, I want to fuck.

I texted him casually, nothing peculiar about that since we hadn't hung out in a while. He said nothing and I told him to facetime me real quick. I barely let it ring twice.

"Hey" I answered with my arm fully extended and the phone angle just low enough for him to see what I did not have on.

"Wassup, you bored huh?"

"Amongst other things, you busy?"

"No, I work a twelve tomorrow so I'm just chillin tonight. What you up to?" He asked while rubbing his hand over his waves repetitively.

I think to myself that's perfect means he won't want to spend the night.

"I wanna fuck." I blurted without ever taking my eyes off the screen.

He stared at the phone, eyes wide without saying a word.

"Hello?" I jokingly knocked on the screen

"Yeah, I'm here but …."

"Let me use my manners, can you come fuck me? Please." Flirtatiously smiling at the camera, hoping to seduce him with my smile.

"If you serious, I can be there in like 30-35 minutes."

"I'll see you in 30 minutes." I ordered before ending the call

Now here I am, freshly showered I lather coconut oil and shea butter everywhere from my chin to my toes. Wearing grey pair of dick me down shorts and a tank top I pulled from the bin I just stuffed when I was "cleaning up". I make myself comfortable on my couch awaiting my company. Listening to music and starting a new board of crockpot dinners on Pinterest until I hear a knock at the door.

Standing at my door smiling like a child who got everything on his Christmas list he kicks his slides off at the door. I turn the sound bar up 5 more notches and walk toward my room.

Once in my room he throws his jacket on the chair where my pile of clean laundry sat an hour before. Leaving his sweats on the floor he mounts my bed in only his black briefs and a condom in hand. I wrap my hands under arms and pull him on top of me. Kissing me while he rubs his hands up my shirt I spread my legs and grant him access to my honey tunnel. He pushes my breast out over the top of my tank and sucks on one nipple while squeezing the other. He trails soothing kisses from the middle of my chest to my belly button ring and while using one hand to pull my shorts to the side he slides one finger inside me.

Kneeling beside me he forces my legs back together and pulls at the bottom of my shorts until they come down to my ankles. With my bare ass exposed he flipped me to my stomach and lifted my ass in the air. Expecting some back shots I was pleasantly surprised to feel his tongue greeting me instead of his dick.

The head was everything I wanted it to be, you could tell he enjoyed doing it. He ate it so good she was throbbing just waiting for him to fuck me to sleep. He rises from his meal and swipes my juices from his face before opening his condom.

Carelessly tossing the wrapper over his shoulder and rolling the armor down his sword before entering my castle.

The first stroke is forceful making his presence felt. The following 3 strokes are equally as aggressive, and I am impressed. I pressed my chest to the bed and put my ass in the air. He strokes me from behind and the strokes are hard but short. He's holding my waist on both sides but every time I go forward to throw it back he slips out. First time wasn't an issue, second time I put it back in myself, but the third time I turned and gave him a look of pure disappointment.

He took that hint and changed positions. I turned on my back, grabbed my toes and held my legs in the air at a 10 and a 2. He hovered over me in a push up position with one hand planted on the side of me as he used the other to guide his dick back inside me. It didn't take long for me to realize this wasn't going to suffice either. It's as if men can only be good at one, if the head is good you should prepare yourself for substandard dickin.

He knew I wasn't feeling it, probably from the fact I hadn't made one noise, since he first put it in. There was one more option before I lost all hope. I scoot until our feet are on the floor and I leave my left leg up on the bed. He immediately started trying to deliver the same inadequate strokes. I stiff armed him and told him to stay right there. I

figured the least he could do was stand there while

I make myself cum. He stood there moaning

louder than me for all of a minute before I felt him

squeeze on my hips and mumble "ohhh fuck". This

nigga came and moments later he went soft!! I

found myself stirring in regret for freeing him from

the friend zone that he sat in comfortably.

Debating internally on if I should pretend I'm not

pissed to salvage his ego and our friendship or if I

should be brutally honest with how unenjoyable

this experience has been. I could see him in the

bathroom examining the condom for leaks before

he flushed it down the toilet. He returns from the

bathroom and with a pitiful look on his face he ask

"you want some more head?" To which I did not

respond because I was already buried in my phone telling my best friend how I wish I just called Chris.

Without hesitation he puts his clothes back on and he whispers "I'll text you" as he heads for the door. I waited for the door to close before I went to lock the door behind him. Turning out all the lights before returning to my bed in complete disbelief. What a waste of a fine ass face, and decent personality. I'm sure some woman, one day will find it in her heart to teach him how to fuck her properly but I am not her.

How will I continue to hang out with him? What if he tells our mutual friends we fucking as if it will happen again? Who has he been fucking thus far and has anyone told him that his sex game needs some work? Does he already know its substandard, and thats why he was okay with the platonic hangouts we had for all this time? I just have sooooo many questions and as I bombard my best friend with these text messages she only responds with laughing faces as if she didn't encourage me to give him a chance. Annoyed and even hornier than I was before because that was just a tease I had to figure out what to do next.

I'm not about to be the girl to have two men inside her in one day but I cannot go to bed like this. Oddly enough I could only think of a Spongebob episode....."Ole Reliable"! I reach over to my night stand pull my wand from its bag. Pink, shiny, fully charged, undefeated and eager to please, there he is. Ten speed Tim.

With no further delay I opened my laptop and scrolled through my favorites to the link for "**tastyblacks.com**". The link took me directly to my faithful "Ebony" "BBC" "Creampie" categories and I chose the forth one from the top. The thumbnail of a brown skin girl bent over a couch was enough for me. The video begins and I lay spread eagle on my bed as I shuffle through Tim's settings. The girl in the video starts whaling out moans just as Tim and I get properly settled.

Tim spins, and shakes as I use my free hand for a piece of penetration. As the stallion on camera strokes the girl I pretend as if he's stroking me. Barely 3 minutes into the video I roll my eyes to ceiling and tip toe into ecstasy.

Soothed by my moans and the way they sing over the sound of the juices Tim has stirred up. I know I'm closer to my orgasm than I was with that grown ass man between my legs. My legs start to tense up so I turned Tim up a notch and let him finish the job…

The nut I received from my battery operated boyfriend was so good it had me wondering why I ever left him alone. Never once has he let me down like men have. Every time I need him he unselfishly serves me and leaves me wondering

why I would ever consider him my plan B.

<u>PLANTED</u>

Nipple rings, oils and things....
Your body is an art that I admire....
Amazed by the way your eyes project all of your
desire

In this place, words are not obligatory
Guided only by your energy, let your hands tell me
a story

Studying your curves until every inch of you I've
learned.... working diligently to ensure your
ecstasy is earned.....

Here is the only place I'll wear shackles....
Slave to all your needs
Collecting nourishment from your garden before I
fill it with my seeds

BITE ME

Taste my fruit basket, know that it's the forbidden kind. Get high off of my presence, can't keep me off your mind.

When it's time to harvest, pick me from the tree. Because after tasting others you'll see none are as ripe as me.

Good for your health, eat me once a day. & when you're tired of taking bites, eat me another way.

Squeeze me properly & I may turn to juice. But eat me passionately and take benefit to the vitamins I produce

Add your banana carefully or multiply in my apples core. While temptation feeds your imagination, & leaves you starving for more.

Bite the apple, let the sweetness that is me roll right off your tongue. Showing you the game has just started, soon as you think you've won.

Triple Double

I'm going to be at the gym all day, with three private training sessions, some pickup basketball games for my own cardio, and instructing two HIIT classes for all interested gym members…. With all of this on my agenda I still mustered up enough energy to have sex at 0430 this morning instead of sleeping a little longer before my alarm went off.

I have to be out of her house in the next hour to get to work on time but being that she sleeps naked I have direct access to everything I want. I roll over and place a kiss on her forehead and two on her cheek before I call out her name. "Demi, wake up baby." I place a brief kiss on her lips in effort not to share my morning breath with her. After receiving no response from my kisses up north I decide to see just how much she can sleep through.

I'm barely able to lick the rim of the honey pot before I hear in a raspy voice "Why are you awake?" I ignore her and continue enjoying my breakfast! With one of her legs straightened out and the other bent at the knee like a number 4 I kiss every piece of her inner thighs. "Isiah" she manages to whimper in between moans.

"Isiah come here" she demands as she pulls on my ears. I refuse to quit, breakfast is ready, and I am starving. I open my mouth and latch it to her body, introducing my tongue and her pussy as if they haven't met before. Diligently, flicking my tongue up and down eventually adding fingers to really get things started. I close my mouth a little and hold only her most delicate part between my lips. I swirl my tongue around her pearl until she breaks open. Calling out my name and pulling at me to come up to her.

I begin kissing her while continuing to play with her clit with my fingers, letting her finish shaking from that first nut before I give her the next one. Morning wood combined with the outrageous surge of horniness I woke up with, make it easier to slip the condom on. She was barely able to fully recover before I was sliding inside of her. Gasping and digging her nails into my shoulder as she opened up for me. Her moans became the lyrics, to the beat my strokes make as I beat deeper and deeper into her. She wraps her legs around me, forcing my body as close to hers as possible. She bites my shoulder blade as I'm drilling my hammer into her box, giving her every inch of me. I assumed she came and the glaze I see when I look down confirms it.

I tried to speed up my strokes in an effort to get mine now but she pushes me back.

"No, let me taste it." She pleads and sticks her tongue out as a welcome sign. I let her up and she doesn't let me down. Immediately she swallows me, I mean the whole thing, gone. "Shitttttt" I exclaimed as she practically sucked all of her juices off of me. Holding the back of my thighs and looking up at me with her mouth opened wide, I grabbed the back of her head and fucked her throat until I came. Letting my nut roll down the back of her throat.

"Good morning, and have a good day." I tell her as I smack her on the ass and rush into the bathroom to take a shower.

Driving 10 miles over the speed limit the entire ride I finally pull into the parking garage. Popping out of their car as I grab my bag from the trunk is none other than my early bird client, Tyler. A slim thick white girl who I would like to say has earned a lot of her shape from hiring me as her trainer.

She was nothing more than bones and boobs when she first walked into my gym seven months ago.

Anyway, the gym has 24 hour access for members but she almost always waits for me in the parking lot so she can pester me with the same question, "what workout have you planned for me today?" We walk in together discussing how I never know what I have in store for her until the workout begins. I find it amazing how she manages to look this good at almost 6 am after I'm sure she worked about twelve hours last night. Still dressed in her grey and teal scrubs, with crocs, and a hospital badge dangling from her neck that reads "RN Tyler Starenski" accompanied by her picture.

"Why aren't you tired, didn't you just get off?" I inquire.

"Yes I did. I'm clenching on to my last pinch of energy just for you."

We walk and debate about the workout I have planned for her private one hour training session today before she hurries off to the locker room to change.

While she changes I unlock my office, the sauna in the mens locker room, and the kickboxing room. I stand outside the women locker room and as soon as Tyler pops her head out I hand her my ring full of keys for her to unlock the women's sauna.

Moments later she returns with my keys and says she can't get the lock open. I ask her to look around and ensure no other women are in the locker room changing before I walk in. She yells all clear and I head toward the sauna only to find it open already. Smiling and topless she summons me with her eyes. Intrigued and confused I manage to spit out the question "What are you trying to do?" To which she frankly responds "fuck you". Here we are standing in a sauna that hasn't been quite kicked on yet, thank God. I'm having a real mental battle with myself on if I should go through with this while she continues taking her clothes off.

This is my business, what if another member shows up this early and happens to see me, the owner fucking one of my clients in the sauna. How would that look? What would this do to the

professional relationship we are forced to uphold

for another 5 months at least? Can I still

effectively train her once we have explored each

other sexually? On the other hand I am a man, and

this woman is offering herself up to me RIGHT

NOW, RIGHT HERE, so of course I want to fuck

her!

I guess it's a good thing she's a nurse at a

women's hospital because I am assuming this roll

of condoms is from work. She rips one off and

hands it to me as she teasingly plays with herself

standing in front of me. I slide it on and bend her

over leaving no time in between because if I

hesitate even a little I might seriously reconsider

what I'm doing. If I am going to risk ruining my business I'm going to fuck the shit out of her and make sure it's worth the risk.

I lay her on the wooden bench, ass hanging off the edge while she holds her legs in the air and her knees are pinned to her sides. I rub my tip up and down against her sugar lips.

I am not sure how I have this much stamina in me seeing as I just broke Demi off less than 2 hours ago but I am working. So much so that my apple watch beeps to let me know I was about to close my move ring, already. I guess she can tell my energy is running out so she volunteers to get on top.

Sitting on her clothes I let her take control. She straddles me with her feet on the seat and her hands on her knees. Grinding back and forth while I squeezed her hips guiding her up and down, we had a good rhythm going. She started slowing down and I knew we needed to speed this up because the longer we go at it the higher the chances of someone walking in on us. I hold her waist and she's using every bit of core and quad strength she's earned to suspend herself in the air while I deliver the deepest strokes I can from beneath her. I wrap my arm around the small of her back and pound her senseless until we both cum.

I pull my gym shorts up and she heads directly to the shower. I slip into a stall to ditch the condom and sneak out of the women's locker room before anyone can see me. I guess that was a sufficient workout for her because after her shower she left.

I went to my office and texted my brother because I had to tell someone how I managed to get off twice, with two different women before most people have even silenced their first alarm for the day.

The rest of my morning was uneventful, so much so that I was able to close my door and take a nap from 9 am until a little after 11. I'm sure I could have slept longer but my brother was here to work out on his lunch break and I needed to tell him all about my morning.

The weight room is relatively empty right now so after we both finish a mile on the treadmill we head in there to do chest and triceps. I'm spotting him for his first set of chest press and telling him all about my wake up round with Demi. He is unimpressed because Demi and I have been a usual hookup since my relationship ended a few months back. Just as he racks his weight I boastfully add how I broke Tyler off in the locker room this morning. He sits up in disbelief.

"Hell no, the quiet, small framed white girl you train in the mornings?"

"Yes bruh, her."

"Hell no, I don't believe that."

"I'll prove it on the camera's if you hurry up and finish this last few exercises."

We power though our workout and head to my office, chopping it up about some random things while we walk. In my office Mike takes a seat while I log in and pull up the camera footage.

"Alright check it out"

He stands behind me with his arms crossed as I open the screen with the camera facing the women's locker room. We see Tyler go in, and come back to the door, then I hand her my keys. She comes back to the door and mike sucks his teeth "man I don't believe this".

I wait until he sees the part where I enter the locker room before I speed the footage up, until I come out 15 minutes later, looking sweaty and suspicious.

"So she _paying_ you to train her _and_ you get to fuck? This got to be the best job ever" Mike uttered enviously.

"Man, you have no idea how bad my nerves was the entire time. Anything could have happened. Plus the sauna was on so it was getting unbearably hot in there. I don't even know how I had the energy to go again because Demi sucked the soul out of me before I left for work."

"You got to play the lottery later because today is your lucky fucking day" he joked

We both laughed and I logged off the computer so I could shower and go get some food.

I shower, throw on some jogging pants from my bag and a clean shirt with my gym logo and contact info on the front and back. I grab my wallet, and head around the corner to Pita Pit. The line is significantly long but that is to be expected during lunch hours. I'm waiting in line, kind of zoned out, when someone behind me taps me on the shoulder.

"Hi, excuse me." I turn around and it is this gorgeous woman. Caramel skin tone and big curly hair, and a very fit build, she is breath taking.

"Hey, whats up?" I respond while turning completely around to give her my full attention.

"I don't want to bother you but are you a member of that gym?" she asks while pointing to my shirt.

I laugh before I can respond "Well I'm kind of a member because I own it" I state proudly.

Her eyes widen and she smiles while smirking in disbelief.

"I'm serious, I'm the owner. Are you interested in joining?"

"I just moved to this area about a month ago and I have been driving past that gym everyday on my way to work."

"Well how about I give you my number, and when you're free I can let you check out the facility and show you all the classes we offer."

She hands me her phone and I create my contact just in time to place my order. As I grab my meal I extend my hand "I'm Isiah Davenport, I look forward to hearing from you…." I pause waiting for her to tell me her name. "Staci" she smiled and shook my hand.

I walk back to the gym, while consuming my entire fruit smoothie. In my office I get comfy at my conference table, eating my food and scrolling down Instagram. When I get the most unexpected notification. A text message from Niyah, my emotionally unstable ex that I haven't spoken to since we broke up over 4 months ago.

"Hey, I know we haven't talked in a while and that's probably for the best. But I really need to see you later. No strings attached." Then a video comes up! Her in the shower, she takes the fingers from her pussy and licks them clean.

I know this conversation can't be had via text so I facetime her. The phone rings a few times before she answers with her air pods in and whispering because she is at work.

"Man, what was that?"

"You know what it is and I'm sure you don't need me to tell you what to do with it."

"We haven't even said hello in months and this is how you feeling today?" I ask inquisitively.

"Yup, and I only need to hear a yes or a no" She candidly responds.

"Can I text you when I know what my schedule looks like for this afternoon?"

"Yes you can, I'll talk to you later." She smiles and hangs up the phone.

Sitting in the chair with my face in my hands, I am in disbelief. How in the fuck is this happening? For about twenty minutes I sit at the table trying to convince myself this isn't as bad of an idea. I've already bust two nuts today, who do I think I am? At this point I'm being greedy, no one man needs this much pussy in one day.

I walk around the gym encouraging a few members through their workout and cleaning off a few machines. Reluctantly I texted Niyah, and tell her I can be there at 6 pm. Hoping that she would change her mind and back out since that was 4+ hours from now.

Before I know it 5:30 rolls around and Niyah sends me another video. She is in the shower again, this time she is covered in soap and all she says is "be here when I get out" then the video ended.

Dammit, she knows I love when her hair is freshly washed and them titties. Needless to say I pack up and head out. Her house is no more than a 20 minutes from the gym and I made it there in 15. I wait on the porch for a second before remembering she keeps a key under one of the flower pots. I find the key and let myself in. I can still hear the water running upstairs and head straight there.

Calling out her name as I walk in the bedroom so she knows that it's me. I open the bathroom door and there's a towel on the counter, which I am assuming is for me. I stand at the door, waiting for her to invite me in herself.

She opens the shower door and immediately I get naked. I'm barely able to get both feet in the shower before her arms are wrapped around my neck. Any other female could not just have her way with me like this and she knows it.

I'm honestly not even sure if my dick will get hard again but we will soon find out. Pressed up against me, kissing me, then kissing my neck I realize I really do need to take a good shower because today was a busy day. I grab the wash cloth she left out for me and lather it with soap. Turning away from her I manage to wash majority of my body, starting with my over worked semi hard dick. Suddenly I feel her hands on my back and she's running her nails down my back and across my shoulders. Damn this woman knows all my weaknesses!!

I turn around and pin her back to wall holding her arms above her head with my left hand and playing with her pussy with my right. Between her and the shower water, all of that splashing woke him right up. We both hate shower sex though, so I give her a little more foreplay before I cut the water off. She steps out before me and sits on the sink. In the mirror I see her sandy brown curls resting on her shoulders and water running down her body. I haven't been this turned on in a long time.

I scoop my arms under her until she is wrapped around my waist. We walk to the bedroom, dripping wet, with our bodies pressed closely together and we kiss until I lay her on the bed. Examining every inch of her, I remember how much I loved this girl. I climb on top of her and with her legs clenched around me, when I realize my dick is standing straight up. I guess he missed her as much as I did.

Laying down until my head is nestled into her neck, I slip inside of her. Immersed in her warm embrace I'm stuck for a second before I manage to start stroking. I had already fucked twice today but I'm not fucking Niyah. The undeniable chemistry between us and the built up of emotions running through both of us make this so much more enjoyable. I pull back and grind smoothly back inside her, over and over again while she claws her nails in my back. Eventually my strokes get deeper as I adjust to being back inside of her. I'm glad I came twice already today because I know this last nut is going to take a while, so I can savor every minute of this.

Supplying strong, deep strokes inside her with one hand on her throat I get lost in the thought of how good we were together. At least in bed, if nothing else. The irrefutable love that lingers between us filled the room with so much passion, frustration and just raw emotion!! Shit is absolutely insane.

I pressed my body against hers again and she bit my shoulder as I dug deeper and deeper inside her. Missionary isn't typically an enjoyable position but boy, I tell you what. The sounds she made as I stuffed my dick inside her had me on a high. My arms are now holding her legs to her sides and she is wide open. I know if I don't change positions soon this will be all she gets from me.

"Flip over" I demanded and she does exactly as I say. Attempting to put her ass in the air I pull her feet down until she is laying flat on her stomach. Spread out like a star fish, I place myself right between her legs and dive as far into her as I can. With my hands pressed down on the small of her back, I go all in. She shoves her face into the pillow and stretches one arm out to slap the headboard.

Every time I go in she squeezes and I can feel her tighten around my dick. That shit drives me insane, it always did. I know she came, I can see it, but I'm not finished yet. I lick my thumb before adding that to the fun. "Ahhhh my goodness" she wailed. I pounced a few more times before standing off the bed and pulling her down to me.

I fucked her from behind, with a whole lot of aggression. As if each stroke was to make up for time spent apart. I know I can make her squirt because I've done it before and I won't stop until I do it again. While she throws her ass at me I play with her clit until she screams. "No, no, no" she pleaded but I was not stopping until I did what I came to do. I committed myself to pleasing her. Vigorously playing with her pearl until I feel her juices running down my leg.

She collapses in defeat and I lay right next to her. Basking in the moment and knowing we cannot make this a regular thing because we cannot get back together.

She gets up to go to the bathroom and I grab my phone from my bag to verify the night shift manager remember to lock the gym up. I see a text from Tyler, Mike, Demi and an unsaved number.

Tyler sent "See you in the morning" with the smirk emoji and I can only hope this woman comes to the gym tomorrow for a trainer and does not spontaneously throw the pussy at me again. Mike asked if I wanted to meet up for food and drinks but that was over an hour ago. The unsaved

number's text read:

"Hey this is Staci, we met on lunch. I was hoping

you could make time for me tomorrow. Around the

same time?" I responded immediately "Of course,

call me when you are outside of the gym."

Lastly, a message from Demi, telling me how she

had an amazing day and she hopes I'll come stay

the night to wake her up like that again tomorrow.

I lay back on the bed in complete disbelief. I'm not

sure what is going on, what stars have aligned to

have all these women pursuing me at once, but I

like it. Shit, tomorrow I'm trying to make it a triple

double!!!

<u>UNTITLED</u>

Roses are red, and violets are blue.
Im trying to see what that mouth do.

Warm in the middle, caution you might slip. Come
up here and kiss me, so I can taste me on your lip.

Ima go til it's soft, can you eat it til I curl my toes?
Hands under my chin, I'll relax my throat, let's see
how far down it goes.

Say it like you mean it and I'll follow every
command. Bend me over the sink and fuck me til I
can't stand.

Using both hands while I'm checking your mic.
Face down in the pillow am I arching I right ?

Feel sorry for your neighbors, I just might be a
screamer. Your skin is dark like coffee & I just
might be your creamer.

UNTAMED

YOU SMELL SOOOO GOOD, BUT YOU TASTE EVEN
BETTER. KEEP ON MAKING ALL THAT NOISE AND
I'LL KEEP GETTING WETTER.

TONGUE TWIRLING IN CIRCLES, I'M YEARNING, BUT I
WON'T BEG. ON MY SIDE, YOU DELIVERING GOOD
STROKES WHILE I'M HOLDING UP MY LEG.

BODY PRESSED AGAINST MINE, I'M HIGH OFF THIS
SENSATION. HOPEFULLY IT'S AS GOOD AS YOU SAY
SINCE WE DID ALL THIS WAITING.

DON'T HOLD BACK, I CAN TAKE IT.
BUT IF IT'S NOT GOOD, I WON'T FAKE IT.

KISSES SO GOOD, THAT THE FEELING LINGERS.
LICK IT UNTIL IT'S DRIPPING AND THEN YOU ADD THE
FINGERS.

SLOW & SLOPPY, THEN I WRAP MY LIPS AROUND IT.
LOOKING FOR THAT SPOT AND WHEN YOUR EYES
ROLL BACK I FOUND IT.

APPOINTMENTS EVERY WEEK, WISH I COULD GO
EVERY DAY. SOON AS I THINK I'VE HAD ENOUGH YOU
DO IT ANOTHER WAY.

THIS FEELING IS EUPHORIC, ADDICTIVE AT THE
LEAST. BUT THIS IS ONLY THE BEGINNING, YOU'VE
AWAKEN THE BEAST

EROTIC REFLECTIONS VOL 2. PREVIEW

Bonus story: The Feast

Mocha brown skin, athletic build, tattoos on every piece of exposed skin, with locs resting on your shoulders, you caught my attention before you even said a word.

You take a seat at the empty chair to the right of Tony and I try not to ease drop as you two catch up a little bit. The party is crowded but miraculously you end up sitting right across from me.

Either she caught the few times I was staring at you or my friend can tell you're my type, because she makes sure to introduce us.

You start to walk away and turn around only to catch me staring, **AGAIN**. You lean down with your face planted directly above my breast, "you want a drink?" You only asked me but I didn't pay that any attention. I was too intoxicated by whatever scent you're wearing. It's familiar but caught me by surprise. Finally I responded, "Yeah, I'll take one"... "oh if you want a drink you have to come with me to get it." This time I'm fully aware that this was a pass at me. I grab my almost empty cup and follow you. The house is unbelievably packed so you cuff your hand around my wrist and lead the way to the kitchen.

I subconsciously chugged my drink in the midst of our conversation. Fixated on the way you lick your lips almost religiously before you start talking I found myself wondering if your lips feel as soft as they look.

Our conversation rapidly turns from harmless flirting to direct sexual innuendos. "Excuse me, what is your name again?" You laugh, "I'm Tommi." "What are you doing in Charlotte, are you from here?" "No I go to school here, so I've been here for almost 3 years now" We hold seemingly harmless conversation and I notice the room is starting to clear out. The host announces that uber's are being called and anyone to drunk to leave can sleep on the living room floor. You turn to ask me what I'm doing after this. I say "Nothing" and look at my homegirls who have obviously forgotten I'm here.

"Come home with me, if you not ready to turn down yet." You look at me, but more like you're looking through me, waiting for my response. "Okay that's fine. I'm not ready to go home and go to sleep anyway."

You never stop looking me in my eyes as you hold your hand out, exposing 3 pills with smiley faces on them, one yellow and two green. I look at you utterly confused by your silent proposition. "Well are you going to take one or just look at them?" "I don't know what that is so why would I take it?" I snap back.

"Calm down babydoll its ecstasy. Nothing that will have you strung out or passed out. It's going to help you get rid of the obnoxious about of nervousness I'm sensing and let me actually get to know the real you. Without any inhibitions."
"Are you taking it too?"
You respond by tossing a green one in your mouth and swallowing it with whatever was left in your cup.

Now to be clear I have taken drugs before but the opposite side of the spectrum. I've sipped a cup of lean through the night and I've sat in my fair share of blunt rotations but I took those to relax, ease my mind. Ecstasy is the drug my college friends took to get wired and go all damn night.

I hesitate for a second processing the endless possibilities of what could happen tonight if I took this and went home with her. Before my brain can actually agree my mouth makes the decision "Give me one". I hold my hand out and put the pill in my mouth and wash it down with what remains of my 4th cup of the community hunch punch bowl. You somehow find two bottles of water and grab them before we head to the door.

We ride back to your house with your roommate and grab some Cookout before we get to your place. Both of us finished our food before we even got out of the car. We barely made it through the door before we started fooling around. We walk in the room, you sit your cup on the night stand before starting to undress.

I sit with my feet hanging off the bed as I watch you take off almost everything. I find it a bit strange that in the past 2 hours you have not once asked me about my sexuality. I'm high as shit now and I don't really want to talk anymore so I'm with whatever you with.

Sitting on the bed alone, I lay back and hit my head on what I believe is the remote control. I flip the cover back to move it only to discover a purple two sided dildo. High as a kite I burst out laughing, flailing the sex toy around like a harry potter wand or some shit. You grab the toy with your right hand and rest the other hand on my thigh.

"Put that down before I show you how to use it."

"what you think I'm scared of you or something because I'm not."

"Good I don't want you to be afraid of me, scary pussy is no fun." You reply in this sexy smart ass tone.

You push me onto my back and climb over me, leaning in for what I think is a kiss. I'm mistaken.

Removing your left hand from my thigh and placing it around my throat you use your thumb to guide my chin to the side leaving my neck entirely exposed. You dance your tongue down from my earlobe to my collar bone and I tense up. "You not scared right?" you ask mockingly.

"Nope" I reply with what little breath I have left in me. "You going do what I tell you?" You inquire. "Only way you'll enjoy this is if you trust me". I nod, signing off my approval for any and everything you want to do to me.

"Take your clothes off" you instruct.

I stand up, wobble to the closet door where I take off my shoes and start to remove everything I wasn't born with.

"When you come back over here bring your belt with you..." you command, in the most seductive way.

I stood there in front of the mirror for a while. Amazed by how liberated I felt. No shame, no hesitation, no overthinking. My body was overflowing with anticipation. I walk back to the bed in my navy blue panties and bra, holding my belt buckle in my fist while dragging the belt behind me.

You stand up and kiss me, briefly, only long enough to have my back to the bed before you scoop me off the ground. Laying me down with my head just below the pillows you place one all but one of them on the floor. Removing the belt from my hand you buckle it around your neck like a dog collar. Placing the long end in my hand you lean in with your lips touching my ears and say "If at any point you can't take it or I'm doing too much pull on the belt as hard as you can. It won't hurt me, and that's the only way I'm going to let up".

Pausing to ensure I'm understanding what you're telling me, I nod slowly. "Say you understand". You ease back waiting on my response before you proceed. I make the decision by placing my hands between you locs and kissing you. You kiss me back and then squeeze my thigh, "Say it!" You demand. "I got it, if I wanna tap out pull the belt. But I'm not going to tap out." I say confidently before you smile and disappear below my waist line.

Clearly there is no rookie setting here because you didn't waste time taking it easy, first timer or not you were taking me for a ride I never imagined. Managing to get my panties down in one swift motion I laid there, wide open to whatever you were about to unleash.

Meticulously tracing your hands over every inch of my body, kissing from my chin to my knees and not missing a single spot in between. You slowly move down to my feet and suck my toes in a way I never expected to be arousing. As if you were summoned by the sound of my second heart beat you returned to my thighs. Playing hopscotch with her lips until you reached your destination.

Coming up for what I hoped was a kiss you grab the cup from the night stand and retrieve a single piece of ice. Balancing that small piece of ice between your lips as you trail it over both my nipples, down my torso, and around my belly button.

Before it completely dissolves against my warm body you place it in her cheek as you lock your lips around my pussy. I flinch not out of fear but because the warmth from inside of me met with the chill of your drastically cold mouth was sensational.

You tango your tongue around my clit while I wrap your locs around my hand. Pulling your hair as you pull the soul out of me. I scream! Calling out to whoever could hear me. I never had head this good. You knew exactly how much licking was enough and how much sucking was too much. Mesmerized by your performance I through my head back in dismay. Why is she doing this to me? What made me come home with this girl? Why hasn't she asked if I'm even into girls? I think to myself as I enjoy the way you're enjoying me.

While I'm staring at the ceiling you used one hand to press down on top of my vagina. Completely confused on what exactly that hand is supposed to do I was caught by surprise when you slipped two fingers from the other hand inside me.

The pointer and middle finger penetrated me expeditiously until my body went stiff.

"Relax, you have to relax" …

So I did just that, I relaxed and felt the flood gates inside of me break open. I've had a plethora of sex, good sex, great sex even and no one has made me squirt. Until today!!! Today you taught me things about my body that I never knew. She showed me a pleasure I have never experienced before this moment. Everything she did to me left me wanting for more.

"You want more don't you?" you ask "I know you do" you respond before I'm able to.

"Tell me what you want."

"I want your roommate to join us" I cover my face with the pillow because I cannot believe I just said that.

You squeeze my thigh, "is that really what you want?"

"Yes!!" I affirm

"Turn over and put your face in the pillow" You instruct and I quickly oblige.

I feel you get up from the bed but I can hear your foot steps and can tell you didn't go far. Interested in where you're going, I take a peak. Only to be met with your gaze and told to put my ass up and keep my face buried in the pillow.

Moments later you return... and with back up. Your roommate has agreed to join us. I'm not sure if this is something that you and her do regularly but I had never been with one female before tonight let alone two. . . . . . TO BE CONTINUED!

Dedication

Once again thank you for supporting my first project. All of my family, friends and social media followers were extremely supportive and encouraging through this entire process and I cannot begin to put into words how much that means to me.

For anyone who reads this who is hesitant for any reason please take this imperfect project as motivation to let nothing, and no one, including yourself hold you back. I have dreamed of publishing a book of my own work for as long as I can remember and for some time I talked myself out of publishing this project out of fear that people would think of me differently, how it make me look as a woman speaking on sex so publicly. Now here it is, I am unapologetically proud of how transparent I was in this book.

Please believe in yourself, you are the only thing standing in your way.

Now if you enjoyed this book, stay tuned because Vol 2 is set to release 1 November 2019.

Made in the USA
Middletown, DE
21 July 2019